The Chest

017

Practising CVCC and
CCVC plus polysyllabic words

First published in 2007 by
Franklin Watts
338 Euston Road
London
NW1 3BH

Franklin Watts Australia
Level 17/207 Kent Street
Sydney
NSW 2000

A CIP catalogue record for this book is available
from the British Library.

ISBN: 978 0 7496 7283 6 (hbk)
ISBN: 978 0 7496 7321 5 (pbk)

Series Editor: Jackie Hamley
Series Advisors: Dr Barrie Wade, Dr Hilary Minns
Series Designer: Peter Scoulding

Printed in China

Franklin Watts is a division of
Hachette Children's Books.

The Chest

by
Sue Graves

Illustrated by
Hannah Wood

FRANKLIN WATTS
LONDON•SYDNEY

Sue Graves
"There was a big chest in my Gran's loft. It was full of old clothes. I had great fun dressing up in them."

Hannah Wood
"I live in a cottage so tiny that it doesn't have a front door! I love painting, my horrible cat called Harry and collecting silly things."

Mum and Bob went to see Gran.

Bob felt sad.

"Can I play in the loft?" said Bob.

"Yes," said Gran.

A chest was in the loft.
It had a lot of stuff in it.

Bob got in the chest.

13

He sank down and down.

"Help!" Bob said.
"I'm sinking!"

Splash! Bob had to swim!

17

He met a pink crab on the sand.

The pink crab ran off.

He met a big fish.

"This is fun!" said Bob.

"I can see a ship,"
Bob said to the fish.

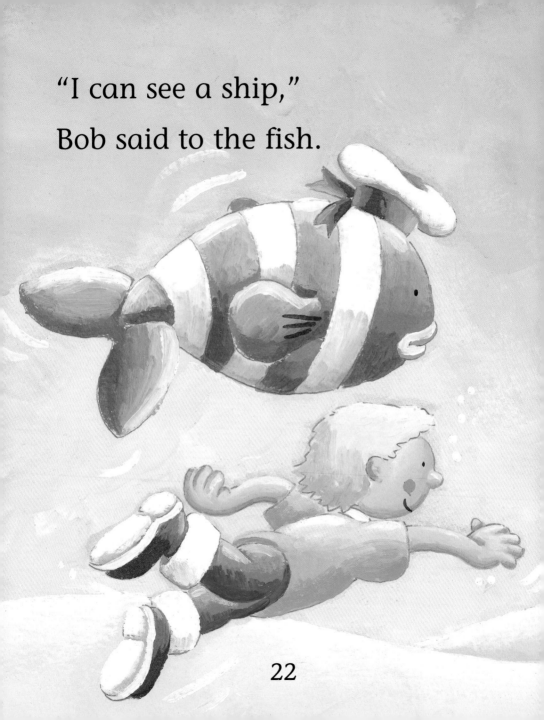

The ship was resting
on the sand.

Bob got a pot. "Gran will like this," he said.

Bob went up and up.

He went to see Gran.

"This is for you!" he said.

"Was that in my chest?"
said Gran.

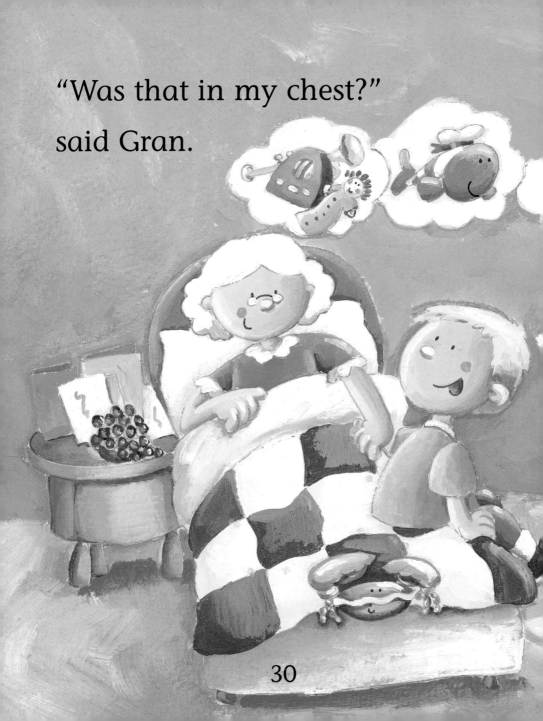

"Yes it was!" said Bob.

Notes for parents and teachers

READING CORNER PHONICS has been structured to provide maximum support for children learning to read through synthetic phonics. The stories are designed for independent reading but may also be used by adults for sharing with young children.

The teaching of early reading through synthetic phonics focuses on the 44 sounds in the English language, and how these sounds correspond to their written form in the 26 letters of the alphabet. Carefully controlled vocabulary makes these books accessible for children at different stages of phonics teaching, progressing from simple CVC (consonant-vowel-consonant) words such as "top" (t-o-p) to trisyllabic words such as "messenger" (mess-en-ger). READING CORNER PHONICS allows children to read words in context, and also provides visual clues and repetition to further support their reading. These books will help develop the all important confidence in the new reader, and encourage a love of reading that will last a lifetime!

If you are reading this book with a child, here are a few tips:

1. Talk about the story before you start reading. Look at the cover and the title. What might the story be about? Why might the child like it?

2. Encourage the child to reread the story, and to retell the story in their own words, using the illustrations to remind them what has happened.

3. Discuss the story and see if the child can relate it to their own experience, or perhaps compare it to another story they know.

4. Give praise! Small mistakes need not always be corrected. If a child is stuck on a word, ask them to try and sound it out and then blend it together again, or model this yourself. For example "wish" w-i-sh "wish".

READING CORNER PHONICS covers two grades of synthetic phonics teaching, with three levels at each grade. Each level has a certain number of words per story, indicated by the number of bars on the spine of the book:

GRADE 1

50 words — CVC words with short vowel sounds

70 words — CVC words plus sounds of more than one letter

100 words — Sounds of more than one letter, simple polysyllabic words

GRADE 2

130 words — CVCC and CCVC plus polysyllabic words

160 words — Long vowel sounds, CVCC and CCVC and polysyllabic words

200 words — Long vowel sounds, trisyllabic words, tricky words